THE PUP'S TALE

PET VET

Book #1 CRANKY PAWS

Book #2 THE MARE'S TALE

Book #3 MOTORBIKE BOB

Book #4 THE PYTHON PROBLEM

Book #5 THE KITTEN'S TALE

Book #6 THE PUP'S TALE

First American Edition 2015
Kane Miller, A Division of EDC Publishing

First published by Scholastic Australia Pty Limited in 2011
This edition published under license from Scholastic Australia Pty Limited.

Text copyright © Sally and Darrel Odgers, 2011
Interior illustrations © Janine Dawson, 2011
Cover copyright © Scholastic Australia, 2011
Cover design by Natalie Winter

For information contact:
Kane Miller, A Division of EDC Publishing
P.O. Box 470663
Tulsa, OK 74147-0663
www.kanemiller.com
www.edcpub.com
www.usbornebooksandmore.com

Library of Congress Control Number: 2014939756
Printed and bound in the United States of America
4 5 6 7 8 9 10
ISBN: 978-1-61067-351-8

THE PUP'S TALE

Darrel & Sally Odgers

Illustrated By Janine Dawson

Kane Miller
A DIVISION OF EDC PUBLISHING

welcome to Pet vet clinic!

My name is Trump, and Pet Vet
Clinic is where I live and work.

At Pet Vet, Dr. Jeanie looks after
sick or hurt animals from the town
of Cowfork as well as the animals
that live at nearby farms and stables.

I live with Dr. Jeanie in Cowfork
House, which is attached to the
clinic. Smaller animals come to Pet

1

Vet for treatment. If they are very sick, or if they need operations, they stay for a day or more at the clinic.

In the mornings, Dr. Jeanie drives out on her rounds, visiting farm animals that are too big to be brought to the clinic. We see the smaller patients in the afternoons.

It's hard work, but we love it. Dr. Jeanie says that helping animals and their people is the best job in the world.

Staff at the Pet Vet Clinic

Dr. Jeanie: The vet who lives at Cowfork House and runs Pet Vet Clinic.

Trump: Me! Dr. Jeanie's Animal Liaison Officer (A.L.O.), and a Jack Russell terrier.

Davie Raymond: The Saturday helper.

Other Important Characters

Dr. Max: Dr. Jeanie's grandfather. The retired owner of Pet Vet Clinic.

Major Higgins: The visiting cat. He has a new home with Tom Ashton. If he doesn't know something, he can soon find out.

Whiskey: Dr. Max's cockatoo.

Magnus: Higgins's friend.

Pipwen: A sheltie mother.

Patients

Tiny: A pup.
Goldie: A yellow Labrador.
Smoke: A sheltie.

MAP of Pet Vet Clinic

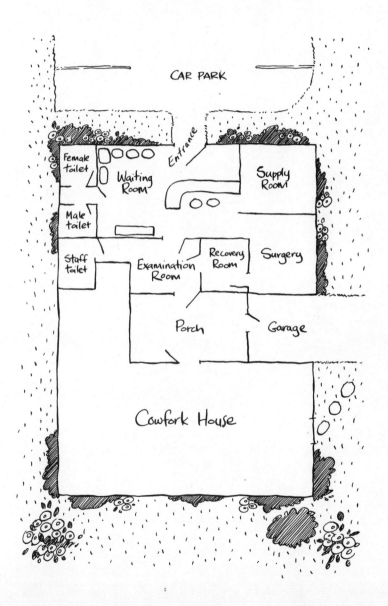

CAR PARK

Female toilet

Waiting Room

Entrance

Supply Room

Male toilet

Examination Room

Recovery Room

Surgery

Staff toilet

Porch

Garage

Cowfork House

Too Many Pups

One sunny Thursday morning, I was doing rounds with Dr. Jeanie. I was surprised when she drove the Pet Vet van to Jeandabah instead of straight to a farm.

I sat up tall so I could see through the van window. We'd stopped in an ordinary street. Maybe someone had a pony or a house cow behind a house? I sniffed at the gap in the window.

Dr. Jeanie looked at her notes. "Number seven," she said. "This is the place." She got out of the van with her bag, and hesitated. "I don't know if you should come, Trump."

I whined to let Dr. Jeanie know that I certainly should come. I am her A.L.O. and I can't do my job if I stay in the van. Besides, I was lonely.

My friend Whiskey had flown off with some wild cockatoos, so I didn't have him to talk to. I also missed Major Higgins. Since he'd found a new home with Tom Ashton and the kitten, Magnus, he hadn't come back to Pet Vet. I tried to tell myself this meant Higgins was happy with Tom. I reminded myself that Higgins always gave me orders, and helped himself to my drinking bowl. A few times, he even stole my kibble. All the same, I missed hunting down his hiding places and playing War Games. I missed arguing with him, too. Terriers enjoy a good argument.

Higgins was helpful sometimes. He had taught me a lot about cats.

I didn't want Dr. Jeanie leaving me alone too, so I wagged my tail and looked hopeful.

"Okay, you can come, but you'll have to be on your best behavior," said Dr. Jeanie. She opened the door and let me jump down. "Come on."

Dr. Jeanie led the way up the path, but before she could knock on the house door, it opened and a girl with messy hair came out. "You're too late," she said.

"Oh?" Dr. Jeanie sounded confused.

"She's had them," said the girl. She looked down. "Hello, Trump. Do you remember me?" I wagged my tail because I recognized her. This was Shaz. We'd met her at Hobson's Farm when the racehorse, Helen of Troy, had her foal.

"I'm **dog sitting** for Madge Winter while she's in the hospital," said Shaz.

"I see," said Dr. Jeanie.

> **Dog sitter—**
> A person who moves into a house to look after pets if the owner is away.

"Madge breeds Labradors," went on Shaz. "I've been looking after them, but Goldie was due to have pups. That's why I called you, because you were so good when Helen had her foal. Only now Goldie's already—"

"I see," said Dr. Jeanie again. "She's had the pups."

"She's in the kennel," said Shaz.

She took us through the house and out to the backyard. I saw something that looked like another house, but one sniff told me dogs lived there. I heard two dogs barking, but Shaz took us into a room with a **whelping box** in it. I sniffed hard and waved my tail as I trotted up to the box. I could smell puppies. I love puppies.

"Careful, Trump," said Dr. Jeanie.

Whelping box— A special box where mother dogs give birth to their puppies.

She was warning me because
mother dogs sometimes get angry
if you get near their pups. I stood
on my hind legs and peeped over
the edge of the whelping box at a
Labrador with a lot of very new
puppies. They all had their eyes
closed. They were wriggling around
and squeaking like baby birds.

"Hello," I said to the Labrador.
"My name is Trump. I'm Dr. Jeanie's

A.L.O. We've come to see you and your babies. There's no need to worry about anything."

The mother dog looked up at me. "That's what you think," she said.

"It's all right," I said. "Dr. Jeanie will tell Shaz how to look after you best so you can care for your pups."

"It's *not* all right," said the mother dog. She nosed at the pups. "I've got this one and this one, and then there's another one here, and some more there. There are too many! I'll never be able to look after them all."

I looked at the pups. They had fat little pink paws and pink tummies. Half of them were a creamy yellow color like their mother. Some were black, and two were chocolate brown. One brown one was the smallest of the litter. I tried to count them, but they were all piled together.

I looked up at Dr. Jeanie and whined.

She was looking at the pups too.

Rainbow litter—
A litter of pups in three different coat colors.

"My goodness, what a big **rainbow litter!**" she said. "Their father is black, I suppose?"

Shaz nodded. "I thought there were a lot," she said. "My aunt's Yorkie had four pups."

"Yorkies are very small," said Dr. Jeanie. "Small breeds usually have smaller litter sizes, but Goldie here seems to have . . ." She began to count the pups, gently touching each on the head. "Fifteen!" she said. "That really is a lot, even for a big dog."

"Goldie is a valuable dog," said Shaz. "Her kennel name is Majestic Golden Madonna. The pups' father is called Majestic Abundance. Madge calls him Abe. These pups will all have **papers**."

Shaz talked on and on while

> **Papers**—A written record of a dog's pedigree.

Dr. Jeanie examined Goldie and the puppies. I told Goldie everything was going to be fine. She didn't listen. She just kept saying there were too many pups and she didn't know what to do.

Trump's Diagnosis. Labrador retrievers are medium-big dogs. They come in three different colors, yellow, black and chocolate. They are popular as pets, and they get along well with other animals. Like most dogs, Labradors need plenty of company. Yorkies, or Yorkshire terriers, are small dogs.

Tiny

When we got home, Dr. Jeanie wrote
up her notes. Dr. Max came in just
as she sat down.

"How's my best terrier girl today?"
Dr. Max bent towards me. I got up
on my hind legs so he could scratch
my ears without having to bend far.
Like old dogs, older humans are
sometimes stiff in the joints.

"She's fine," said Dr. Jeanie. "We
saw a new patient today; a Labrador
with a rainbow litter of fifteen pups.

She belongs to Madge Winter."

Dr. Max raised his eyebrows. "Fifteen! Are they all thriving?"

"It's too soon to tell," said Dr. Jeanie. "The pups seem healthy, but one is a lot smaller than the others."

"There's often a **runt**," said Dr. Max.

Dr. Jeanie smiled. "Trump's brother Preacher was smaller than his sisters when he was born and look at him now!"

> **Runt**—The smallest pup or piglet in a litter.

Dr. Max chuckled. "Preacher's mother had only four to look after. Some bitches with big litters give all their attention to the bigger pups."

"Hmm," said Dr. Jeanie. "I might check in on them in a couple of days.

Madge is in the hospital and Shaz from Hobson's Farm is looking after her dogs."

"I know Shaz," said Dr. Max, grinning. "She talks all the time, like Whiskey. Jeanie, if you see Whiskey, let me know. I miss the old bird. It's not like him to be gone for so long."

"Have you been to look for him?" asked Dr. Jeanie.

"There's not much point, since he can fly. I suppose he'll be back when he's ready," said Dr. Max, before going home.

It was time for the clinic, so Dr. Jeanie finished writing her notes and opened the doors for the patients.

My mind kept wandering back to Goldie. I know mother dogs can be a bit anxious when they have new pups. Goldie seemed more than a bit anxious. I hoped Shaz would look after her well.

I cheered up when our friends Donna and Terri came in with their senior dog, Terdona Smokey Mountain. Smoke is a **blue merle** sheltie. He's what Dr. Jeanie calls a gentleman dog.

Blue merle— A coat color with mixed shades of gray and a bit of tan and white.

She means he is polite and well-mannered.

"Hello, Smoke," I said. "How are you feeling now?"

"I'm quite well, young Trump," said Smoke. "My stitches itch a bit, that's all."

Dr. Jeanie had removed a **cyst** from Smoke's shoulder on his last visit. He had come to have his stitches taken out.

Cyst (sist)— A lump under the skin that is usually filled with fluid.

He waved his long plumy tail, and then sat down next to his owners to wait for his turn. He calls Donna and Terri his "ladies," so I sometimes call them that too.

I knew I didn't need to reassure him about the clinic, but I sat beside him. I wanted to ask his advice.

"Smoke, you know a lot about puppies, don't you?" I said.

Smoke stared at me. "Of course. I am a father and grandfather many times over," he said. "My pups are always fine and healthy."

"How many pups do mother shelties have?" I asked.

"Four to six is a good litter size," said Smoke. "But my daughter Pipwen has a litter of three. My ladies were surprised."

"I saw a Labrador this morning with fifteen."

Smoke turned his long nose towards me. "Fifteen is a lot of pups," he said. "Pipwen could not feed that many." He must have seen I was worried, because he said kindly, "But you can't compare Labradors with shelties, Trump. Labradors are bigger dogs. They are also retrieving dogs. We shelties are herding dogs. And of course you Jack Russells are . . . ahem . . ." He looked embarrassed.

"We're quarrying dogs," I said. "We were bred to dig up fox dens and to chase rats."

"Quite so," said Smoke. "All dog breeds have their own special talents."

Dr. Jeanie called the ladies in then, and Smoke went calmly into the examination room. I didn't follow, because it would be quite crowded in there with three humans and Smoke. Instead, I sat down to think about Goldie and her pups. I was worried.

It turned out that I wasn't the only one worried. Dr. Jeanie usually has a day off on Sundays, but this week she rode out to Jeandabah on Dr. Max's old putt-putt. I rode in the dog box on the back.

"I hope Shaz doesn't think I'm interfering," she said as she took off her helmet.

I trotted up the path ahead of Dr.

Jeanie and nipped off to the kennel. Three other dogs were exercising in the yard. I let myself in by squeezing under the gate. A half-grown black pup came dashing up and asked me to play with him, but I told him I had to see a patient.

"Don't go near Goldie," he told me. "She tried to bite my nose."

"She won't bite me," I said. "Is Goldie your mother?"

"Oh no," said the pup. "I was born a long way away. I came here on a plane. My name is Hereward Tessa's Challenge. I have a very long pedigree." He bounced around behind me. "Do you have a very long pedigree?"

"No," I said. "I don't need one."

"Why not? I need one."

"You need one because you are going to be a show dog," I explained. "I don't need one because I am not a show dog. I am an A.L.O."

"You mean you are just a common dog," said Challenge.

"That's right," I agreed. "There's nothing wrong with being a common dog."

I left the pup to think about that, and went to see Goldie. When I peeped into the whelping box, she was lying on her side, feeding some of her pups. She had one of the black ones between her front paws, and she was licking his tummy.

"Hello," I said,

Goldie stopped licking the pup

and looked at me. "I have a lot of pups," she said.

"I know," I said. "They're beautiful."

"I have too many," she said. "Would you like one?"

"You have fine pups," I said, "but I couldn't look after them. I have never had any myself, so I have no milk to give them."

"I don't have enough for all of them," said Goldie. "I can nearly do it, but not quite. That one has to do without." She looked over her shoulder.

I ran around to the other side of the box. Most of the pups were cuddled up against Goldie, but one of the brown ones was all alone behind her.

I looked down at him. He was

smaller than the others and he was just lying there.

That's how I first met Tiny.

Trump's Diagnosis.
If mother dogs don't have enough milk to feed all their puppies, it is usually the smallest one that goes without.

CHAPTER 3

Majestic Overflow

"You can't leave him like that," I said to Goldie. "He needs food."

"I don't have enough milk," said Goldie. "I have too many pups. Would you like one?"

Tiny opened his pink mouth and made a sad little squeak. Like any baby, he couldn't really talk yet, but I knew he was crying for food.

I jumped into the whelping box and gave him a nose-over. He was cold. I couldn't feed him, but

I could keep him warm. I curled around him. "It's all right," I said. "I'll look after you."

But of course I knew I couldn't.

"Trump? Tru-ump?"

I pricked up my ears. Dr. Jeanie was calling for me. I whined to let her know where I was. After a moment I heard her outside, talking to Shaz.

"I expect she's gone to look at

Goldie's pups again," said Dr. Jeanie. "How is she managing that big litter?"

"All right, I think," said Shaz. "I gave her plenty of extra food and water. Madge told me what to do. There seems to be one pup she doesn't like much, though."

"Oh?" said Dr. Jeanie. Shaz and Dr. Jeanie came in and leaned over the box. "There you are, Trump!" said Dr. Jeanie. "What are you doing?"

"She's got one of the pups," said Shaz. "That's the one Goldie doesn't seem to like. I'm a bit worried about it."

"Hmmm." Dr. Jeanie bent lower. "Hello, Goldie," she said gently. She patted Goldie, and then picked up Tiny. He squeaked again.

"This fellow isn't doing so well, is he?" said Dr. Jeanie.

I whined to let her know I agreed.

"He's quite **dehydrated**," said Dr. Jeanie, pulling gently on the pup's loose skin.

Dehydrated (de-HIDE-rated)— Dried out.

"Oh dear," said Shaz. "Is there anything you can do for him? I have tried to get Goldie to look after him, but the others push him away so he doesn't get much to drink."

"You could keep trying," said Dr. Jeanie, "but she has so many she probably *can't* manage. You could try feeding him with a **syringe** or eyedropper, but it isn't easy. He'd have to be fed several times a day, and massaged so he feels as if someone is looking after him."

> **Syringe**
> (s'RIN-j)—
> Plastic tube for giving medicine or injections.

"But he's so small," said Shaz. "Can you look after him at the clinic?"

"No," said Dr. Jeanie. "I wish I could, but I have a practice to run. My grandfather's hands are too stiff to feed a pup this young."

"I could try hand-raising him," said Shaz, "but I'm more used to big animals."

"There's something else we might do," said Dr. Jeanie. She put Tiny back in the box and he cuddled up against my belly. I licked him. "We might try him with a foster mother."

Shaz clapped her hands. "Trump could do it!" she said. "That's a great idea! She's looking after him already."

Dr. Jeanie sighed. "No, Shaz. We'd need a mother dog with very young pups." She sighed again. "You should talk to the breeder and find out what she wants to do. Some people prefer not to invest too much time and trouble with litter runts."

"I'll call Madge right now," said Shaz.

Shaz rushed into the house, leaving Dr. Jeanie with me, Goldie and her litter.

Dr. Jeanie stroked my shoulder. "We do get ourselves into some situations, don't we, Trump? Maybe we should just let this pup take his chances with his mother."

I didn't think that was a good idea. I could hear the other pups sucking milk and grunting happily. Tiny was crying.

After a bit, Shaz came back. "I talked to Madge. She asked which pup it was, and when I said it was the chocolate boy, she said someone had put in an order for him when he's old enough. In the meanwhile, she'd like to try a foster mother. She said if she was feeling well enough she would telephone other breeders to find one. Then she said

> **Nursing bitch—** Mother dog who is feeding her puppies on her own milk.

maybe *you* know someone with a **nursing bitch**."

"I do know of one," said Dr. Jeanie. "She's not a Labrador though, she's a sheltie. That's a Shetland sheepdog."

"But that's great!" said Shaz. "If she's a different breed, Overflow can't get mixed up with her own pups!"

"*Overflow*?" said Dr. Jeanie.

Shaz nodded. "That's what his pedigree name is going to be. Majestic Overflow."

Trump's Diagnosis. Purebred dogs with pedigrees usually have fancy names. These names start with their stud name, or kennel name. Goldie's real name is Majestic Golden Madonna, so all her pups have to have "Majestic" at the beginning of their names. Because these names are often long, the dogs have an everyday name too.

CHAPTER 4

PiPWEN

I was pleased to hear Dr. Jeanie's idea. Donna and Terri must have told her about Pipwen's small litter while she was taking out Smoke's stitches.

Dr. Jeanie telephoned the ladies to explain what had happened. I couldn't hear what they said, but they must have agreed right away. Dr. Jeanie wrote down the details for Shaz to give Goldie's owner, and picked up Tiny.

"Come on, Trump," she said. I followed her back to the putt-putt.

Dr. Jeanie fastened my harness and put Tiny in the dog box. "You look after him while I drive, Trump," she said. I curled around Tiny again. It was the best way to keep him warm. I talked to him as we puttered along. He couldn't hear me, because pups can't see or hear when they are very young, but he knew I was there.

We went back through Cowfork and pulled up next to the Terdona kennels.

Dr. Jeanie tucked Tiny into the front of her jacket and knocked on the door. Several dogs barked a polite challenge.

"We are the Terdona kennel pack. Who goes there?"

"It's me, Trump," I replied through the door. "May I come in?"

The Terdona shelties are all very polite dogs, so I had to be polite to them.

"Coming!" called Terri. Dr. Jeanie and I stood back as she opened the door. Nine shelties crowded forward to greet us. They were a mixture of blue marles, **tri-colors** and **sables.**

> **Tri-color**—A dog with a coat made up of three colors: black, white and tan.

"Back up, girls," said Smoke. He was behind the others, but they did as he said. Dogs that live alone with humans have human pack leaders. (My pack leader is Dr. Jeanie.) But dogs that live with other dogs usually have a top dog *and* a human pack leader. Smoke is the top dog of the Terdona shelties.

> **Sables**—Dogs with a mix of golden-brown coat color.

Donna and Terri were talking to Dr. Jeanie, but I was kept busy greeting the shelties. They crowded around me until I was almost buried in a mass of long flowing coats and plumy tails. Long noses came forward to sniff me all over. Shelties aren't much bigger than I am, but they have so much hair they *look* bigger. I knew they were friendly, but I felt my hackles trying to rise. Being surrounded always makes my hackles itch.

"Girls, outside now," said Donna. She opened the back door and most of the shelties trotted out to their exercise yard. Smoke stayed in with us. He was watching Dr. Jeanie.

"Dr. Jeanie has a puppy," he said. "Why has she brought a puppy here? Is it sick?"

I was explaining about Tiny when Dr. Jeanie and the ladies went through to a quiet, warm room. I followed.

"This is the whelping room," said Donna. "Most of the shelties have their own beds in the kennel house, but we keep new mothers in here so they can have some privacy."

Smoke pattered in front of us and led the way to a whelping box well-padded with blankets and soft towels. "This is my daughter, Pipwen, and her pups," he told me. "Their father is Hurrydown Jasper Six. He doesn't live with us."

Pipwen was a pretty sable dog. She was curled around three fat puppies. She looked up at us and waved her tail. "Hello, Trump," she said to me. "Dad told me he saw you at Dr. Jeanie's. Do you like my pups?"

I waved my tail back. "They're fine pups," I said. "You are looking after them well."

"I am a good mother," said Pipwen. "This time, I have two girls and a boy." She licked one of the girl pups lovingly. Then she looked up at Dr. Jeanie. "What's she got in her jacket? Have you had puppies too, Trump?"

"No," I said.

Pipwen sniffed. "But that one smells like you."

"That's Tiny," I explained. "His mother can't look after him. He smells like me because I have been keeping him warm. We hope you might give him some milk."

Pipwen looked doubtful. "I have my own litter to look after. And that isn't a sheltie."

"He's a chocolate Labrador," I said. "But he's really hungry. He needs a dog mother to feed him and teach him all the things puppies have to know."

"Hmmm," said Pipwen. "I don't

know much about Labradors. They're not like us. They're big dogs. They do big-dog things."

"Tiny is a very *small* big dog," I said.

While Pipwen was still thinking about it, Donna picked up one of the towels from the whelping box. Dr. Jeanie handed Tiny to her, and she rubbed the towel gently over his coat. "She might accept him if he smells like her own pups," she said. She put Tiny into the box.

Pipwen reached out her long nose and sniffed Tiny. "He isn't fat. Pups should be fat," she said to me.

Tiny cried weakly.

"He'll soon get fat if you give him some milk," I said.

"Oh, all right," said Pipwen. She

nudged Tiny down by her belly and gave him a couple of licks. "I have enough room for another one."

I wagged my tail. "You're a lifesaver, Pipwen," I said. And I really meant it.

Dr. Jeanie had a cup of coffee with the ladies. I had a drink of water and then went to talk to Pipwen again. She didn't have much to say, but I liked watching Tiny getting what he needed. He drank milk until he had had enough, and then he snuggled down with the sheltie pups and went to sleep.

Pipwen cleaned up all the milky little faces. Then she looked up at me. "Four is a nice number of pups," she said. "And he's looking a little bit fat now, don't you think?"

He was. I felt really pleased. Dr. Jeanie came in to look at the pups again and smiled. "I think this will work, Trump," she said.

I agreed.

Trump's Diagnosis. Some animal mothers will feed babies that are not their own. This is called "fostering." Cows do it, and so do cats. Occasionally they will even feed a different species of baby animal.

Unexpected Visitors

We had a busy week. Shaz called us
out to check on Goldie and her litter
again. This time, Goldie seemed
more settled. We didn't stay long,
because we had other patients.

On Wednesday, Cordelia
Applebloom brought Dodger into
the clinic. He was wet through and
snuffling sadly. Dodger is a healthy
border collie who is always having
little accidents. This time, he had
fallen into Cordelia's new fishpond

and swallowed a lot of water. He coughed most of it up in the waiting room.

I was glad to be busy, because I felt lonely. Whiskey was still visiting the wild cockatoos. Dr. Jeanie and I heard him squawking in the hills above Cowfork township, but he hadn't come home. Whiskey and I are old friends. He's the one who taught me about being an A.L.O., so I really missed him.

I was pleased when Tom Ashton pulled up outside the clinic in his Petstuff Products van just as Dr. Jeanie closed the doors on Friday. He hopped out of the van and ran to our door with his case of samples.

"Wait!" he called.

Dr. Jeanie smiled. "Nice timing, Tom. I'm about to have a cup of tea. Would you like one?"

"I would," said Tom. He bent to pat me. "How are you, Trump?"

I wagged my tail. Tom is the sort of person everyone is pleased to see. Besides I wanted news of my friends Higgins and Magnus.

> **Caterwauling—**
> A loud squalling sound cats make when they're annoyed, or challenging other cats.

"Have you found any more stray kittens?" Tom said to Dr. Jeanie.

"No," she said. "Why? Did you want another one?"

Tom grinned. "No thanks. Magnus and Major keep me busy. Magnus has taken to **caterwauling** on my stone wall. It annoys the neighbors."

"You should keep him inside at night," said Dr. Jeanie.

"I try," said Tom. "But that kitten can get out of anything. Major is as bad."

"Major," said Dr. Jeanie. "That's a good name for the old boy."

"It goes well with Magnus," said Tom.

Dr. Jeanie took Tom through the clinic and into Cowfork House where we live. She gave me kibble and made the tea. "Apart from the caterwauling, how are you getting on with Major and Magnus?" she asked. "Have they settled in?"

"They're great," said Tom. "I like having cats around. They make a place feel like home." He opened his sample case and pulled out some brochures. "I can recommend these stable cat bowls with confidence. Major and Magnus have one each and they're easy to clean. They're stackable, too." He beamed. "They come in six different colors."

Tom and Dr. Jeanie went on talking about Petstuff Products as I finished my kibble. I was about to settle down for a nap when I heard a **distress call**. I let myself out through the

Distress Call—A call given by dogs or other animals when they need help or advice.

dog door and trotted off to find out who was in trouble. I was heading down Shady Lane when something

caught my eye. I looked up and saw
a half-grown kitten hanging by his
front paws from a low branch. It was
young Magnus.

"Magnus!" I said. "Are you all
right?"

Magnus kicked in the air a few
times and swung himself onto the

branch. He peered down at me. "Hello, Trump!"

"That is not protocol, Private," said another voice. "You shouldn't have broken cover."

"Hello, Higgins," I said. "What's wrong?"

Higgins peeped down from his hiding place on a higher branch. "At ease, Trump."

I found myself sitting in good dog position, with my front paws together. Higgins was doing it again!

"Nothing's wrong," said Higgins.

"We wanted to talk to you," put in Magnus. "So Major Higgins made a distress call. He said that would draw you out without alerting Dr. Jeanie." He flipped his tail. "I don't want to see Dr. Jeanie. She might put me in a cage again."

"She'd get Tom to take you home. Come down," I said.

"Should we, Major Higgins?" asked Magnus.

"Check for enemy forces first," said Higgins.

Magnus looked up and down the lane, and then swarmed down the tree. He rubbed his whisker cushions against my nose.

I sneezed.

Higgins came down too, and **head-bumped** me.

Head-bump—A friendly butt cats give people and animals they like.

"Good to see you too, Higgins," I

said. "I hope you haven't run away from Tom."

"Why would we do that?" asked Magnus. "We *love* Tom. We love his friend Felicity too. She looks after us when Tom is away. And we love—"

"That's enough, Private," said Higgins. He cuffed Magnus lightly across the head. "Our present living quarters are very good," he told me. "However, we make **sorties** now and then."

> **Sorties**—Trips out and about.

"We challenge other cats and conquer territories," said Magnus. "I nearly fell into a fishpond just now. A dog called Dodger told me he did fall into it."

I hoped Higgins wasn't getting

Magnus into trouble. They both looked well, though. Higgins was sleek and healthy and Magnus had grown. "How did you get here?" I asked. "And *don't* say that's classified. Did you come by train?"

"We came with Tom," said Higgins.

"Only he doesn't know," said Magnus. "We stowed away under the old blanket in the back of the van."

"But we'll go home on the iron horse," said Higgins. "Otherwise Felicity will be worried." He puffed out his whisker cushions. "A sensible cat never worries his humans, Trump. Remember that."

"No," said Magnus. "If humans get worried they start locking the cats in cages."

"Warrrrk!" said someone else from the top of the tree.

Magnus, Higgins and I all peered upwards. We saw Whiskey looking down.

"Whiskey, you'd better go home," I said. "Dr. Max misses you."

"Who's that?" asked Magnus.

"That's Whiskey," explained Higgins. "He used to be the A.L.O. at Pet Vet."

Whiskey climbed down to hang upside down from the lowest branch. He looked hard at us through his beady eyes. "I'm on my way home, Trump," he said. "Flying with a flock is all very well, but there's no sunflower seed in the wild. What's been happening?"

"Yes, what?" asked Higgins.

It was just like old times. I settled down and told my friends all about Goldie, Pipwen, Smoke and Tiny.

Trump's Diagnosis.

Cats with good owners usually stay at home, but some cats like to wander. It is difficult for an older cat to change its habits.

SUPPER WITH THE LADIES

Things improved for me the next week. Whiskey was back with Dr. Max, and I knew Higgins and Magnus would visit again. On Saturday, Davie took me for a long walk after work. And then on Sunday, Dr. Jeanie took me to supper with Terri and Donna.

Smoke and the other shelties greeted me, and this time, Pipwen was with them.

"I have been for a run in the

yard," she told me. "Now I have to get back to the pups." She trotted back into the whelping room and I followed. The pups were in a pen now. They were asleep in a pile on a thick layer of newspaper. They woke up as soon as Pipwen arrived.

"Mum! Mum! Mum! Mumma Pip!" they whined, and scrambled towards her. They were walking

quite well, and they all had their
eyes open. Their little tails stuck out.

Soon all four of them were settled
to feed. The three shelties already
had long silky coats like their
mother. It was easy to pick out Tiny.
He was darker in color and his coat
was shorter. He was still small for a
Labrador, but he was bigger than the
shelties.

When the pups had had enough
milk, Pipwen washed their faces.
They waddled over to the edge
of the pen and made puddles on
the newspaper. Then they started
tumbling around, giving shrill little
growls.

Tiny rolled over and waved his
fat paws in the air. Then he caught

sight of me. "Who's that, Mumma Pip?" he asked.

"That's Trump," said Pipwen. "She's a friend, so be polite."

"She looks funny," said Tiny. "Why does she look funny? Where's her plume and **feathers**?"

> **Feathers**—Some dogs and horses have long hair on their legs. This is called "feathering" or "feathers."

"She looks funny because she's a smooth-haired Jack Russell terrier," said Pipwen. "Smooth-haired Jack Russells don't have plumes or feathers."

I asked Pipwen's permission and then hopped into the pen. I gave Tiny a gentle nose-over. "Do you remember me, Tiny?" I asked. I wasn't sure if he would remember or not.

Tiny sniffed at me. His nose was pink, like his paws. "Sort of maybe," he said. He sniffed me again. "You're the warm one," he said. His little tail waggled.

"That's right," I said. "I kept you warm when you were very, very little."

"You were nice," said Tiny. One of the sheltie pups got up on her hind legs and tumbled over Tiny's shoulder, and soon he was back playing with the other pups.

"He's happy," I said.

"My pups are *always* happy," said Pipwen.

I didn't point out that Tiny wasn't really her pup. She was looking after him and teaching him manners just as if he was.

Dr. Jeanie and the ladies came to see Tiny and the others, and Dr. Jeanie smiled.

"Have you heard from this fellow's breeder?" she asked.

"Yes," said Donna. "She's out of the hospital, but she asked if we could keep the Lab pup on until he's weaned. There doesn't seem much point in putting him back with his own litter now, especially since she has to go back into the hospital in a few weeks."

Dr. Jeanie lifted Tiny out of the pile of puppies. He wriggled and licked her fingers. "He's doing very well," she said. "Have you started them on **solids** yet?"

"We thought we might start them today," said Donna.

Donna and Terri mixed milk with

> **Solids**—Like human babies, puppies are fed on milk to begin with, and then begin eating mushy food called "solids."

some ground-up rice. They put this in a shallow plate. Donna called Pipwen and me out of the pen and set the plate near the pups. They kept playing for a while, and then one of the shelties wobbled over to the plate. She sniffed at the mushy rice, and then licked it.

"Yummy," she said. She sucked
up a mouthful and sneezed.

Tiny tried some too, but he put his
feet in the dish. Soon he had milky
rice all over his paws and tummy.

"I think that's enough," said Terri.
"Pipwen will clean up the mess. In
you go, Pip."

Pipwen hopped back into the pen
and began to clean the pups. She
was so busy I don't think she even
noticed when Dr. Jeanie and I left.

Trump's Diagnosis.

Raising puppies is a lot of work for the mother dog. It's a lot of work for the human owners, too. The pups and their pen need to be kept clean. The pups also need **socializing** before they're weaned.

Socializing (soash-al-ize-ing)— Being introduced to people and other animals so they'll be friendly and confident.

CHAPTER 7

What Labradors Do

The next time I saw Tiny, he was
eight weeks old. By then, he was
weaned and running around.

The ladies brought him to Pet Vet
along with the three sheltie pups
for a checkup before they went to
new homes. I was delighted to see
him again. He had come a long way
since he was a sad, hungry little
baby. This time he
remembered me
right away.

"Hello, Trump,"

> **Weaned**—No
> longer living
> on milk.

he said, and reached up to lick my
nose. I licked him back and we
played a little game of prance paw.

"Overflow's breeder wants to pick
him up next week," said Donna.
"She checked on him last month,
but then had to go back to the
hospital for follow-up treatment."

"Next week's a bit of a problem,"
said Terri. "We're taking these three

to new homes tomorrow. Pipwen is tired, and we don't want to leave just the one pup with her. So—"

Dr. Jeanie smiled. "So you'd like us to board him at Pet Vet for a few days?"

"It would solve the problem," said Terri. "It would be good socializing for him. We don't want to be a nuisance, though."

"We can manage now that he's weaned," said Dr. Jeanie. "And I got you into this."

The ladies laughed. "It's been interesting," said Donna. "He's a dear little dog."

"Maybe you should leave him with us today," said Dr. Jeanie. "I'll put him in a puppy pen. Trump will look after him."

The ladies gathered up the three shelties, hugged Tiny, and went away.

It was a sunny day, so Dr. Jeanie put Tiny in a pen in the backyard of Cowfork House. Then she went to finish off some work. Of course, Tiny started to cry for his foster family.

I jumped into the pen with him. "It's all right," I said. "I know you're lonely now, but I'll keep you company while you're here. After that, you'll go to a new home."

"Mumma Pip said I would have a forever home. What sort of home?" asked Tiny.

"I don't know, exactly," I said. I remembered what Challenge, the black pup, had said the day Dr. Jeanie and I rescued Tiny. "You have a pedigree," I said. "You might be a show dog."

"What's a show dog?"

"A dog that goes to shows and tries to win prizes," I said. I don't know much about show dogs, so I couldn't explain any more.

Dr. Jeanie came out later to give Tiny some puppy food. He had learned not to put his feet in the plate, and he didn't get much food on his face. He wagged his tail and grinned at Dr. Jeanie. He had been well brought up. Well, that's what I thought then!

After he had eaten, Tiny had a nap. He was still snoozing when Dr. Max came up the lane with Whiskey on his shoulder.

"You're puppy sitting, I see," said Dr. Max to me. "Maybe you can cockatoo sit this bad bird as well."

He took Whiskey off his shoulder and put him on our fence. "You stay there, Whiskey," said Dr. Max.

"Huh," said Whiskey. He ruffled his feathers and stretched one wing. I noticed the **flight feathers** had

> **Flight feathers—**
> Long feathers
> at the edge of a
> bird's wing.

been cut short.

"Don't stare, dog," said Whiskey crossly. "I can still fly." He ruffled his wings above his head. "I just can't fly very far. Dr. Max is making sure I stay near home for a while."

I didn't say anything about that.

I knew Whiskey would grow some new flight feathers after his next **molt**.

Whiskey sidled along the fence. "What pup have you got there?" he asked. "Is

> **Molt—**
> Shedding fur or feathers and then growing new.

he a patient?" Whiskey is always interested in our patients, because he used to be the Pet Vet A.L.O. when Dr. Max ran the practice.

"That's Tiny," I said. "I told you about him the day you came home. He's strong and healthy now."

"I can see that," muttered Whiskey. "But is he friendly?" He fluttered down from the fence and settled next to me, just as Tiny woke up.

Tiny yawned and stretched his little pink paws and his tail. Then he saw Whiskey. Before either of us could say anything, Tiny scrambled out of the pen. He stumbled and fell on his nose, then jumped up and bustled towards Whiskey.

"Warrrrk!" squawked Whiskey. He sidestepped and almost fell on his tail feathers.

Tiny sidestepped too. He gave

a few little yaps, and rushed at Whiskey.

Whiskey squawked with shock and dodged.

Tiny yapped again.

I jumped between Tiny and Whiskey. "Tiny! What are you doing?" I snapped. "You mustn't chase Whiskey!"

"I'm not chasing. I'm practicing my herding," said Tiny.

"Your what?" I asked.

"Mumma Pip taught us all about herding," said Tiny. "We run back and forth and we make ducks an' sheep an' things go where we want. Mumma Pip says that's important." He peeped past me to look for Whiskey.

"But you're not a herding dog!"

I said. I moved to block his view while Whiskey made for the fence.

Tiny peeped around me again. "Mumma Pip explained all that," he said. "She says shelties are made to be herding dogs. She says the ladies don't need us to herd stuff, but we should know how to do it." He tried to bounce past me to get at Whiskey.

I put my paw gently on his head. "Sit," I said. I gave him a firm stare.

"But I want to herd the bird," whined Tiny.

"The bird doesn't want to be herded," I said.

"But that's what shelties do. Mumma Pip said."

Whiskey had reached the fence and I heard him climbing out of reach. I took my paw off Tiny's head. "Shelties are herding dogs," I said, "but Tiny, you're not a sheltie."

"But Mumma—"

"Be quiet, pup. Listen to Trump," squawked Whiskey. He was back on the fence, preening his feathers into place.

Tiny stared up at him. I've never seen a pup look so surprised. "That bird knows dog talk!" he said.

"Yes," growled Whiskey. "I am an educated bird. I speak all kinds of animal **dialects**. I taught Trump to speak them, too." Then he looked at me. "Trump, that pup has been brought up as a sheltie. Someone has to teach him what Labradors do."

> **Dialect** (die-a-lect)—A different kind of language.

Trump's Diagnosis. During their first weeks, pups learn a lot from their mothers. They learn how to behave with other dogs. When they are weaned, pups are ready to go to new homes. They still need a lot of looking after, but they no longer need their mothers. Their new human owners have to teach them the rules of their new homes.

CHAPTER 8

LaBraDor Lessons

"Does it matter if he acts like a sheltie?" I asked. "Shelties are nice dogs."

"He is a Labrador," said Whiskey. "Remember, Trump, Tiny is going to a home where the people will expect him to act like one. You will have to give him Labrador lessons."

"Oh," I said. "How?"

"If you were teaching him Jack Russell lessons, what would you do?" asked Whiskey.

I thought back to when I was a pup

myself. Mum Jill Russell and Dad Jack gave us lots of lessons. "There's staring," I remembered. "Jack Russells are very good at staring."

"No good," said Whiskey. "Terriers and herding dogs stare. Labradors are retrievers."

"We learned to bounce and bark and bustle. And to dig. And to chase."

"Yes," growled Whiskey. "As I recall you wanted to grab my tail when we first met."

"Do I have to learn all that?" asked Tiny.

"No," I said. "You can learn to retrieve. Do you see that ball over there?"

Tiny looked across the grass at my ball. "Yes," he said.

"Run and get it," I said. "Bring it back to me."

Tiny ran off across the lawn. He picked up the ball and ran back to me, then put it down. "Very good!" I said. "That's retrieving."

I scooted the ball with my nose. "Get it again!" I said. Tiny was already on his way.

"This is fun!" he yapped when he came back a second time. "Again, Trump, again!"

I scooted the ball harder. It was a while since I'd had another dog to play with.

"Labradors are water dogs," said Whiskey after a while. "Where's the nearest water?"

"The fishpond at Dodger's place, I suppose," I said. "Dodger fell in it, and Magnus nearly did."

"That'll do," said Whiskey. He launched himself off the fence and flapped off towards where Dodger lives with Cordelia Applebloom. I knew we probably shouldn't go there without Dr. Jeanie, but sometimes an A.L.O. has to make quick decisions. And I decided Tiny's Labrador lessons were important.

"Dodger?" I called from outside his gate. "May we come in?"

"Who's we?" asked Dodger. "I warn you, there's a dangerous fishpond in here. It's taken my chew toy."

"It's Trump and Whiskey from Pet Vet," I said. "And we have Tiny with us. He's having Labrador lessons."

Tiny and I crawled under the gate, and Whiskey clambered over it. Dodger gave us a nose-over (and nearly got his nose pecked by Whiskey) and then led the way to the backyard. "Cordelia Applebloom is out shopping," he said. "I have to guard the fishpond and make sure no one—"

A loud splash interrupted Dodger's explanation. Tiny had jumped into the water and disappeared.

I was about to jump in after him when he popped up to the surface. He paddled his paws and swam back to the edge. "Look, Trump! Look what I can do!" he spluttered.

I stared at him. Bits of stick bobbed around on the pond, and I saw Dodger's chew toy bouncing around on the waves.

"Again!" said Tiny. He bounced around and jumped back into the pond. Water splashed everywhere. Dodger gave a howl of dismay and backed away. Tiny swam across the pond and grabbed the chew toy in his jaws. He swallowed some water, but paddled back with his chin held high.

"I did it," he said, dropping the chew toy on the grass. "I retrieved!" He pushed the toy back into the water and bounced after it.

"That's my toy!" said Dodger. "Give it back!"

I bounced around on the edge of the pond. I didn't want to swim myself, but I found myself barking and prancing. After all, I am a Jack Russell. Dodger soon joined in, and

Whiskey perched on the back gate,
flapping his wings and squawking
with laughter.

We were making so much noise
none of us heard the front gate

open. Then Cordelia Applebloom,
Dr. Jeanie and Dr. Max all came into
the backyard.

"Oh, Dodger! You're all muddy!"
said Cordelia. Dodger wagged his
tail and looked sheepish.

"Whiskey, you're a bad bird!"

said Dr. Max. Whiskey flipped his tail feathers.

And Dr. Jeanie just stared at me. Jack Russells are experts at staring, but I found out then that vets are even better.

Dr. Jeanie fished Tiny and the chew toy out of the pond. She tucked Tiny under her arm and apologized to Cordelia. "I hope he hasn't scared your fish too much," she said.

"*I* just hope he hasn't swallowed any," said Cordelia. "Just think, if brave Dodger and Trump hadn't given the alarm, that poor little mite could have drowned."

"Hmmm," said Dr. Jeanie. "I don't think there's much fear of that, Cordelia. Overflow is a Labrador, and they love water. I see I should have put him in

a more secure pen." She clicked her
fingers to me. "Come along, Trump."

"And you, Whiskey," said Dr.
Max. He picked Whiskey off the gate,
and we all went home. Dr. Jeanie and
Dr. Max were laughing.

A few days later, Madge Winter came
to Pet Vet. She said Goldie was well,
and her other pups had all gone to
new homes. "And now it's time for
Overflow to go as well," she said.

"I hope his new owners appreciate
him," said Dr. Jeanie. "He's a fine
little dog."

"He's a lucky little dog," said
Madge. "And I'm sure his new
people will love him. They have a
two-year-old yellow Lab and they
particularly wanted a chocolate

male. They live out in the country near a lake, so I hope this boy likes water."

"Oh, he likes water," said Dr. Jeanie.

I was sorry to see Tiny go, but it sounded as if he would have a good home. And that's something all pups need, whatever kinds of dogs they grow to be.

Trump's Diagnosis. It's important to fit the right kind of pet in the right kind of home. All pets need food and water, and a warm, safe place to sleep. Some don't need a lot of company or attention, but others do. Some need a lot of room to run around. Others don't. Before you get any kind of pet, make sure it will fit in with the kind of home you have to offer. That way, you and the pet will both be happy. Another important thing to remember is that pups grow into larger pups, and then into grown-up dogs, but they still need lots of love *and attention*.

ABout the Authors

Darrel and Sally Odgers live in
Tasmania with their Jack Russell
terriers, Tess, Trump, Pipwen, Jeanie
and Preacher, who compete to take
them for walks. They enjoy walks,
because that's when they plan their
stories. They toss ideas around and
pick the best. They are also the
authors of the popular *Jack Russell:
Dog Detective series.*